TWO TO TANGO

A NATALIE STORY

Book design by Jake Nordby
Illustrations by Jomike Tejido

Published in the United States by Jolly Fish Press, an imprint of North Star Editions, Inc.

First Edition
First Printing, 2018

This is a work of fiction. Names, characters, places, and incidents are either the product of the author's imagination or are used fictitiously, and any resemblance to actual persons living or dead, business establishments, events, or locales is entirely coincidental.

Library of Congress Cataloging-in-Publication Data (pending)
978-1-63163-153-5 (paperback)
978-1-63163-152-8 (hardcover)

Jolly Fish Press
North Star Editions, Inc.
2297 Waters Drive
Mendota Heights, MN 55120
www.jollyfishpress.com

Printed in the United States of America

TWO TO TANGO

A NATALIE STORY

KELSEY ABRAMS

ILLUSTRATED BY JOMIKE TEJIDO

TEXT BY WHITNEY SANDERSON

JOLLY FiSH PRESS

Mendota Heights, Minnesota

Chapter One

The moment Natalie saw him, it was love at first sight. He gazed back at her with his expressive dark eyes. It felt as if she'd been waiting for him all her life . . .

He tossed his head and whinnied anxiously. Natalie hurried forward and took his lead rope from Liz, a volunteer from the Sugarberry Animal Shelter. She noticed a gold nameplate gleaming on his leather halter: Tango.

"What's his story?" Natalie asked Liz, reaching up to stroke the horse's long, elegant neck. He was big—at least sixteen hands—with a splashy brown-and-white coat and a thick black-and-white mane and tail.

That would make him . . . Natalie tried to picture the chart of American Paint Horse coat patterns from her *Horse Breeds of the World* book. *A bay tobiano*, she remembered. Paints were a pretty common breed in Texas. Lots of kids on the junior barrel-racing circuit rode them. The farm even had another Paint, Picasso, who had been rescued from a neglectful home.

But unlike many of the animals that came to Second Chance Ranch, this horse looked healthy and well cared for. In fact, he was gorgeous.

Liz seemed to sense Natalie's surprise. A college pre-vet student who volunteered at the shelter, Liz had delivered animals to the ranch before. "I know. Not your typical rescue, right?" she said. "But we got a call a few weeks ago from somebody who saw this guy wandering in the woods on the road near Ingotts'."

Natalie shuddered. Ingotts' Farm was well known for buying up horses and cattle as cheaply as possible and auctioning them for a profit. Many of the animals there ended up going to slaughter. Second Chance Ranch had saved horses from Ingotts' before. Natalie only wished they could rescue them all.

"But how did a horse like this end up there?"

Natalie wondered out loud as Tango lowered his head to sniff at Autumn, the calico barn cat who thought it was her job to greet every new visitor to the farm.

"Beats me," said Liz, resting her hand on the gelding's muscular hindquarters. "Most of them are in a pretty sad state by the time they get to Ingotts'. The folks there claimed that this guy belonged to them, but they couldn't come up with any papers or proof. So he's been living at the shelter for the last few weeks. But as you know, we just don't have the facilities to keep horses long term. Luckily, this guy's got a clean bill of health from our vet—nice manners too," she added, smiling as she watched Autumn rub her head against the curious horse's nose.

Then she glanced down at her watch. "Shoot, I was supposed to pick up a pony in Sassafras Springs half an hour ago. You need a hand with this guy first?"

"Thanks, but I don't think so," said Natalie. "My sisters are getting his stall ready, and my dad's around somewhere in case there's any trouble. Tango seems pretty calm, though. Not like that mustang you brought us a few months ago!"

Liz smiled. "I know he'll be in great hands here. And as always, call if you need anything!" The young woman gave Natalie a quick wave, then got into the cab of the Sugarberry Animal Shelter's pickup truck, with its paw-print logo on the door. Soon, the truck and trailer were rattling down the ranch's long driveway.

"Hey, Natalie!" Her nine-year-old sister, Grace, appeared in the doorway of the big oak barn across the yard. "The stall's all ready for the new horse. I used three wheelbarrows-full of shavings so he'll have a nice, soft bed if he wants to lie down after his trip."

"Looks like you got most of the shavings on yourself," said Natalie, laughing at the sight of her sister's jodhpurs and T-shirt covered in a dusting of woodchips.

Grace combed through her long blond hair, and a shower of them rained to the ground. "Yeah, the wind was kind of blowing in my direction between the shed and the barn," she admitted.

Natalie led Tango into the barn, where Grace showed her to the prepared stall. The fluffy shavings were piled high, and there was a fresh flake of hay in one corner. Natalie's other sister, Emily, hung a brimming bucket of water from a hook on the wall.

Emily let out a little gasp of surprise when she saw the new horse. "Oh, he's so pretty! What's his name?"

"Tango. At least, that's what his halter says," said Natalie.

"Is he friendly?" she asked, hesitating before reaching out to pat him.

"Seems to be," said Natalie.

Emily stroked the horse's soft nose. The big Paint snuffled her affectionately, like he had with Autumn, then nibbled at the end of her blond ponytail.

"That's not hay, silly," said Emily with a giggle, pulling her hair free.

It was a good thing Grace and Emily wore their hair differently. A lot of people had trouble telling them apart otherwise. Although Natalie had no difficulty knowing which of her twin sisters was which, they had fooled everyone at school once by switching clothes and hairstyles for a day.

But you couldn't spend much time around Grace and Emily without seeing the differences between them. Emily was as careful as a cat, while Grace was as bold as a leaping Labrador. Still, they had both changed a lot since they'd been adopted into the Ramirez family three years ago. Emily was more willing to try new things, and Grace had learned to stop and think before acting—sometimes.

Speaking of sisters . . .

"Where's Abby?" asked Natalie. At twelve and a half—the oldest of the four girls—Natalie did her best to keep the others out of trouble between the time when they got out of school and their mother got home from Sugarberry Animal Hospital, where she was a veterinarian. Their dad worked around the ranch, but he was often out running errands or busy with a million other things.

"She's in the kennel, of course," said Emily. "You know she's not crazy about horses like we are, and she can hardly tear herself away from Cocoa's puppies."

Natalie wasn't surprised. Abby spent pretty much every spare minute with the ranch's rescue dogs—and even more now that Cocoa the cocker spaniel had given birth to six adorable puppies.

That reminded Natalie to update the Second Chance Ranch blog later that night. The puppies wouldn't be old enough to adopt for another month, but hundreds of people had followed the story of Cocoa's rescue from an abandoned building scheduled for demolition. They were sure to be curious how she and her puppies were doing.

Right now, though, Natalie needed to get Tango settled into his new home. He followed her willingly into the stall. The other horses were outside, where they spent all day and sometimes clear nights roaming the farm's fifty acres of pasture.

Natalie slipped off Tango's halter and stepped back. He circled the stall a few times, pawing at the deep bed of shavings. Then he craned his head high and whinnied loudly. Natalie heard a distant reply from one of the horses in the pasture.

"He seems a little restless," said Emily.

"Can't we let him out to run around with the herd?" asked Grace.

"We don't know how he'll act around other horses

yet," said Natalie. "We can let him out later, when Mom and Dad are around." Natalie's parents trusted her with a lot of responsibility for the animals, and she tried to think carefully before making any decisions.

Grace looked disappointed, but Emily nodded in agreement. They watched as Tango circled once more, then lowered his head with a sigh and grabbed a mouthful of hay.

"Anyway, thank you for getting his stall ready, but now it's homework time," said Natalie.

The girls were allowed to ride and help in the barn for an hour after school. Then it was study time until dinner.

Emily put away the wheelbarrow, hung up her pitchfork, and headed inside without argument. Grace hung over the half-door of the stall and watched Tango eating his hay.

"The pattern of his coat looks like a map, doesn't it?" she said. "I wonder if he was treated badly by his last owners, like Picasso. But he's got such a nice halter with his name on it, so I guess someone loved him once. Do you think we can ride him?"

Grace had a habit of asking more questions than anyone could answer at once—especially when she was supposed to be doing something else.

"Look, he's got shavings in his tail already," she went on. "Our teachers barely gave us any home-work today, so I'll just give him a quick grooming before—hey!" she cried as Natalie pried her off the stall door.

"Tomorrow," said Natalie. "Right now, you need to study for your math test."

"How'd you know I have a math test?" she demanded.

"Emily said so."

Grace sighed. "Of course she did." She made a face and then trailed reluctantly off toward the big white farmhouse.

Natalie lingered for a moment outside of Tango's stall. It was her night to cook dinner, and she needed to make sure Grace actually did her homework and Abby hadn't gotten so wrapped up with the puppies that she'd forgotten her other chores. But it was hard to tear herself away from the new horse. Grace was right—his coat *did* look like a map of a mysterious, unknown land.

Natalie wished her best friend, Sophia, were here to see Tango. Sophia loved horses, but she had moved to Boston six months ago. They still talked and texted as much as they could. But it was hard to keep up with half a continent between them.

Natalie whistled a few notes. Tango looked up from his hay and stepped forward to sniff at Natalie's outstretched hand. She smoothed his long forelock out of his eyes, revealing a perfect white star in the middle of his chestnut forehead.

Natalie had outgrown her old pony, Rockette, last year. She'd sold her to the family of an eight-year-old girl who was already winning a lot of junior barrel-racing prizes with the quick little mare—just like Natalie had done since she was eight.

Natalie had been hoping to find a bigger horse to show this summer, but none of the rescues that had come to Second Chance Ranch since then seemed like the right fit. And Natalie didn't want to buy a fancy show horse and take up space that could be used to help an animal in need.

But Natalie was sure that Tango would be as wonderful to ride as he was to look at. She could already picture herself on him, galloping down the chute of a rodeo arena and circling the barrels at lightning speed.

Natalie gave Tango a final pat, then switched off the lights and headed for the house. It really did seem like she'd finally found the dream horse she had been waiting for.

Chapter Two

"Is it spicy?" asked Emily, sniffing cautiously at her bowl of steaming chili. Natalie loved fiery food and so did Grace, but the other sisters weren't so crazy about it.

"Shouldn't be too bad," said Natalie with a grin. "I only used two habanero peppers and one ghost pepper this time."

Abby dropped her spoon. "Natalie!" she wailed. "I can't eat this."

"I think your sister's kidding," said Mr. Ramirez, raising an eyebrow at Natalie.

"Yeah, Abby, I was just joking," Natalie said quickly.

Ten-year-old Abby was on the autism spectrum. She was super smart and very literal. She didn't usually get sarcasm. Sometimes it was hard to resist teasing her, but Natalie didn't want her to be too upset.

"The only spices I used were garlic, oregano, paprika, and a tiny bit of red chili powder," she assured her sister.

Abby picked up her spoon again, looking relieved. "That's good," she said. "I didn't want to have to eat a peanut butter and jelly sandwich for lunch *and* dinner."

Even though Natalie would have loved to have used more than a pinch of chili powder, she'd wanted to make a dish that everyone would enjoy. Dinner was often the only time in the Ramirez family's hectic day that all of them were in the same place at once. And since they were all eating from the beautiful pottery plates that Natalie's abuela had made, it sort of felt like she was there, too, even though she lived in New Mexico.

The family tradition was that everyone went around the table at dinner and told a little bit about their day. Tonight, Mr. Ramirez went first. "I'm glad that we seeded those fifty acres next to the big pasture for hay," he said. "It was a lot of work, but the price of round bales has nearly doubled this year. We'll save a lot of money this winter by feeding the horses hay we've grown ourselves."

As she got older, Natalie realized more and more how expensive it was to keep a place like Second Chance Ranch running. The family organized fundraisers several times a year, and sometimes they got money from government grants. But her parents still tried to keep costs down however they could.

Lately, a lot of their donations had come from people online who had seen the Second Chance Ranch website and blog. Natalie was usually the one who updated the website, and she felt proud that her pictures and writing were making a real difference for the ranch.

Natalie's thoughts were interrupted by Mrs. Ramirez's funny story about an escaped cat at work. Then she took a second helping of chili, which Natalie noted with satisfaction. When she'd first started making dinner once a week, she hadn't exactly been *Top Chef* material. There may have been a few scorched pots and possibly one tiny visit from the fire department . . .

But since she'd started following her abuela's handwritten recipes and calling her grandmother if she had any questions, Natalie's cooking had gotten a lot better.

She noticed that Emily wasn't eating much, though.

"Too spicy?" Natalie asked.

"No, it's good," Emily said softly. "I guess I'm just not that hungry. I had kind of a frustrating day."

"Me too," said Grace.

Mrs. Ramirez shushed her and said it was Emily's turn to talk. "Why was it frustrating?" she asked Emily.

"Because Braden Parker borrowed my colored pencils without asking during art class, and he broke one."

"Which color?" asked Abby, who had somehow separated the corn from the ground meat from the kidney beans in her bowl of chili and was eating each ingredient one by one.

"Turquoise," said Emily with a sigh.

"That's a bummer," said Abby.

"Yeah, she nearly cried," said Grace. "But don't worry, Emily, you can take that pencil out of my set because I don't really use them much. Even if I did, I'd still give it to you because I know how much you love drawing."

Emily cheered up at that and took a big bite of chili.

"My day was frustrating because I spent most of today's soccer game on the bench," said Grace.

"How come?" asked Mr. Ramirez.

"Because I told Jade that a sack of oats could block more goals than she blocked today. Which happens to be true, but whatever."

"Maybe you'd get to play more if you spent more time kicking the ball and less time providing commentary," said their father.

"I know, I know," muttered Grace around a mouthful of buttered cornbread.

"I had a great day," said Abby. "I played with each of Cocoa's puppies for ten minutes to help socialize them. And they finally have names. I decided to name them all after powdered spices that can be used in baking, like Cocoa. So they're called Nutmeg, Cinnamon, Ginger, Clove, Cardamom, and

Cayenne—you should like that one, Natalie. I made name tags for them so that everyone can tell which one is which."

Natalie half-listened to Abby chattering about the puppies, but she was still thinking about Tango, imagining all the prizes they could win at barrel racing this summer. She gazed dreamily into her glass of milk and then realized that everyone was staring at her.

"How was your day, Natalie?" Emily prompted.

"I had—well, it was a good day," she said. "Because of the new horse."

Natalie's father nodded. "I stopped to check on him on my way in. He seemed a little restless, but that's nothing a few days out with the herd in the Texas sunshine shouldn't cure. We can let him out tomorrow."

"Can I try riding him after school?" Natalie asked her parents.

"I don't see why not," answered Mrs. Ramirez. "Liz said he doesn't seem to have any injuries or behavioral problems. But we still don't know him yet, so be careful and make sure someone else is with you."

After supper, Natalie let Abby drag her off to see the puppies while Emily and Grace washed the dishes. As always, Abby was accompanied by Amigo, her ten-year-old golden retriever. Amigo wasn't just a pet; he was also a trained service dog.

Abby's autism made it hard for her to communicate her feelings and to tune out things that most people could just ignore—like loud noises or bright lights. When Abby was younger, she used to get so overwhelmed that she would just start crying and rocking on the floor, and nobody knew how to help her. It had been really hard for her to go to school.

But that changed when Abby got Amigo. Amigo was able to warn her when she started to show signs of being overwhelmed, like rocking in her seat or flapping her hands. Abby had learned to turn her attention to Amigo instead of retreating into her own head and letting her anxiety get worse and worse.

These days, people might not even know that Abby had autism. Anyone meeting her for the first time might notice that her voice was sometimes kind of flat or had a funny singsong tone. Sometimes when she got anxious, she would hum to herself or flap her arms. But mostly, she just acted like any other ten-year-old with a dog obsession and a very analytical mind.

The kennel was a big room in the back of the house, with a dozen fenced-in dog runs outside. Cocoa and her puppies were in a big pen in the corner, with a fleecy bed and a scattering of dog toys. The puppies had been resting with their mother, but they woke up and began romping all over when Natalie and Abby entered the room. They were still so small that

they often went tumbling into somersaults when they tried to run.

"Now that they have names, I can make a pet profile for each of them," Natalie said. Each adoptable animal at the ranch had its own page on the website, with photos and information about its age, breed, health, and personality.

Natalie took a picture of each puppy with the camera on her phone. "You'll have to tell me more about their personalities," she said to Abby. "I've been so busy with the horses that I haven't spent much time with the puppies."

"Cayenne is already the alpha dog," said Abby, picking up the reddish-brown puppy that was running in excited circles around her feet. "She wants to be the boss, and she nips at the others if they get out of line. She reminds me of you, actually."

"Thanks a lot," said Natalie, laughing.

"You're welcome. Cinnamon is kind of gentle and kind of sleepy, but she loves attention." Abby picked up a soft brown puppy and kissed it on the head before setting it back down. Abby paused to scratch Cocoa behind her chocolate-colored ears before grabbing a black puppy that was trying to escape over the wall of the pen.

"And this is Clove," she said. "He's the adventurer of the litter and very independent. He'd be good for someone who likes to be outside and has a lot of room for him to run around."

One by one, Abby explained each of the other puppies' personalities. Natalie stayed to play with them for a few minutes, then went upstairs to her room and wrote a blog update. She ended with: "The puppies will be ready for adoption in just six weeks, so stop by during our open-house hours on Saturday if you want to meet them!"

Natalie wondered if she should add something about Tango. She decided to wait until she had some pictures of him. When she was riding him tomorrow, maybe Emily could take some; she was the best photographer in the family.

Natalie really wanted to share the news about Tango with Sophia too. Somehow, Natalie had gotten so busy that they hadn't talked in more than a month. Natalie pulled out her phone and texted her. Sophia didn't reply. Could she be mad at Natalie for some reason? Could she have forgotten her? Then Natalie remembered the time difference. It was already after eleven o'clock in Massachusetts.

It was getting late in Texas, too, so Natalie closed her laptop. She could hear Emily and Grace whispering in their room across the hall, even though they were supposed to be asleep by now. Abby's light was already out; she liked to go to bed early and wake up before everyone else.

After Natalie said good night to her parents, who were reading downstairs in the living room, she got ready for bed. Autumn was already curled up in one corner of the bed, purring.

Natalie switched off her overhead light and turned on the reading lamp beside her bed. The lampshade was gold, with a black silhouette of a barrel-racing horse that cast a shadow on the wall.

Natalie picked up the book she was supposed to read for English class, but she soon found her mind wandering. She stared at the dark outline of the horse leaning into the turn around the barrel, its rider sitting tall in the saddle.

Natalie missed barrel racing. The speed, the thrill, the feeling of connection with her horse . . . She loved all the horses and ponies on the farm, but she didn't have a special bond with any of them like she'd had with Rockette.

Until now, maybe?

Natalie fell asleep dreaming of the wind in her hair as she and Tango rounded the third barrel and galloped for the finish line. They crossed it in the fastest time for any junior barrel racer . . . the fastest time that anyone had ever seen.

Chapter Three

Natalie walked into English class the next morning and found a new girl in the empty seat beside hers—the one Sophia had always sat in. Natalie felt a flash of irritation and then realized how silly she was being. It wasn't like Sophia was coming back.

Ms. Coleman introduced the girl to the class. "This is Darcy Chang, and she just moved here from Hawai'i. Let's all give her a warm Texas welcome, okay?"

Darcy waved to the class and said a soft hello. She looked a little shy, but her outfit was as bright as could be: a hot-pink denim jacket over a shirt with a silver wave design. Her short black hair was cut in an asymmetrical style, and her glasses had metallic-pink frames.

Pink wasn't exactly Natalie's favorite color. In fact, she was pretty sure she didn't own a single item of pink clothing. But on this girl, it somehow worked.

Ms. Coleman passed out worksheets and told everyone to pair up. Their assignment was to write about the motivation of the characters in the book *Holes* by Louis Sachar. Natalie had thought the book looked interesting when she'd read the back cover

last night. Unfortunately, she hadn't gotten much further than that.

Natalie glanced around and saw that her usual friends had already paired up. Meanwhile, Darcy was fiddling with a button on the sleeve of her jacket, looking a little uncomfortable.

"Hey, do you want to work together?" asked Natalie, waving to get the girl's attention. It must have felt awkward to be the only new kid in a sea of unfamiliar faces.

"Sure!" said Darcy, sounding relieved. She scooted her chair closer and took a fancy ballpoint pen and a new notebook out of her stylish-looking backpack.

"First, I have to apologize, because we're not going to get a very good grade on this assignment," said

Natalie. "I kind of got distracted by stuff instead of doing the reading last night, so I have no idea who any of these characters even are."

"That's okay. We already read this book for class at my old school," said Darcy. "It's pretty good, actually."

"Really? You're the best! How about you tell me everything you remember about it, and I'll tell you everything you need to know to survive the year at Sugarberry Middle School."

Darcy smiled. She wore braces with pink brackets that matched the frames of her glasses. "It's a deal," she said.

With Darcy's help, they filled out the answers on the worksheet in just a few minutes. Then they chatted while the other pairs finished the assignment.

"I like your haircut and glasses," said Natalie. "Actually, your whole outfit is cool. You look like you should be on one of those top-teen-model shows on TV or something."

"Thanks," said Darcy. "That's my dream—but as a fashion designer, not a model. Someday, I want to go to design school in New York City. So far, I've only ever lived in Hawai'i, and now here."

"What's Hawai'i like?" asked Natalie. She thought it sounded like a glamorous place to live, although she wondered if there were many horses.

"Oh, it's beautiful," said Darcy. "My mom and I lived in Pearl City on the island of Honolulu, but my aunt's house is right on the beach, and we visited a lot. I miss surfing and swimming already."

"Yeah, there aren't too many beaches in central Texas," said Natalie wistfully. She lowered her voice a little as Ms. Coleman scanned the room to see who was finished with the assignment and who was still working.

"Do you have any brothers or sisters?" Natalie asked Darcy.

"Nope, it's just me and my mom. My parents are divorced, and my dad still lives in Hawai'i. What about you?"

"Three sisters. Abby's ten, and Emily and Grace are twins. They're nine."

"Is it fun having a big family?"

"Most of the time. Except on pizza night, when everyone else seems to get the toppings they want, and one of my sisters always gets the last slice. I'm telling you, Abby's like a hawk going in for the kill if there's pepperoni involved."

Darcy giggled. "At my house, I only have to compete with Cleopatra. She's my cat, and she's spoiled rotten. Do you have any pets?"

"Yeah, about fifty of them," said Natalie casually.

"*Fifty*?" Darcy's eyebrows shot up.

"My family runs an animal rescue on our 200-acre ranch," Natalie explained. "We've got horses, cats, dogs, goats, chickens, and a couple of rabbits right now. Oh, and a potbellied pig named Portobello."

"That sounds amazing," said Darcy, her eyes wide. "Cleo's the only pet I've ever had."

"Maybe you could come visit sometime," Natalie offered.

"That would be great. I don't know many people here yet, and I—" she stopped as Ms. Coleman signaled to get everyone's attention.

They spent the last fifteen minutes of class discussing the answers everyone had given on the worksheet. When Ms. Coleman called on Natalie and Darcy, Darcy answered for both of them.

At lunch, Natalie and Darcy sat together. Darcy told Natalie more about Hawai'i, and Natalie told her all about the teachers and the quirky old school building. Natalie wished that when she had started middle school, someone would have informed her about the bathroom near the gym that was almost definitely haunted. Or about the corner of the science lab that still smelled funky from a beaker of sulfur someone had dropped behind the radiator a couple of years ago.

Natalie also pointed out to Darcy which of the boys in class were terminally obnoxious—and which were more or less civilized.

"Who are *they*?" asked Darcy, glancing over at two girls on the other side of the cafeteria who were having a loud conversation, complete with dramatic hand gestures.

"That's Riley and Danica," said Natalie flatly. "They're, um . . . probably not the right people to give you a 'warm Texas welcome.'"

Riley and Danica weren't bullies or mean girls, exactly. They were just . . . well, they made Natalie think of two little dogs running around and nipping at everybody's heels. The two girls seemed to do whatever they thought would make people look at them, even if it only got them scolded. And they were always getting into arguments and gossiping behind each other's backs. Natalie didn't think they'd be very good friends for Darcy—or anyone, to be honest.

Darcy seemed grateful for the advice, and Natalie was glad she'd decided to give the new girl a chance. Natalie had fun hanging out with a lot of the kids at her school, but she hadn't been really close with anyone since Sophia moved away.

Part of Natalie liked the idea of having a new best friend in Texas. But Natalie and Sophia had promised not to let distance come between them. Sophia had always been beside her, and something didn't feel right seeing Darcy in Sophia's place. Plus, you could only have one best friend at a time. Otherwise, it didn't really mean anything.

On the bus ride home, Natalie checked her phone and saw that Sophia had texted her back:

Definitely!! It's been way too long. Talk to u at 5:30 tonight (ur time)?

OK! Natalie replied. At first she could hardly wait, but suddenly, she remembered Darcy and wondered just how much of her day she actually wanted to tell Sophia about.

When Natalie headed out to the barn later that afternoon, Emily and Grace were already putting bridles on their ponies, Joker and Bluebonnet.

"Do you want us to wait for you?" Emily asked, leading Bluebonnet out of her stall. Meanwhile, Grace struggled to get feisty Joker to accept the bit instead of clenching his teeth like a toddler refusing to take a bite of applesauce.

"That's okay. You go on ahead, and I'll meet you in the arena," said Natalie. She helped Grace get Joker's bridle on, slipping her finger into the corner of Joker's mouth so that it was open long enough for her to slide the bit between his teeth.

After Emily and Grace finished tacking up, Natalie found Tango out in the pasture with the other horses. He was standing on a ridge a little apart from the rest of the herd.

His neck was arched, and his ears pitched forward as he looked at something in the distance. The wind blew back his two-toned mane and tail. The sight was so striking that Natalie just stood there, watching him for a moment. Then she took her phone from her pocket and quickly snapped a few pictures.

When he saw her crossing the windswept expanse of pasture, Tango let out a high-pitched whinny. He spun on his hindquarters and loped over to meet her. Some horses were difficult to catch, but Tango practically shoved his head into the noseband of his halter. Once again, Natalie noticed what a nice halter it was, coppery-red leather with its polished-gold nameplate.

"Guess you're ready to get to work, huh?" she said to Tango as she led him inside the barn. "But first, you're going to get the official welcome with our Second Chance Ranch grooming experience."

She crosstied Tango in the wide concrete aisle and put together a new grooming kit for him from the bucket of spare brushes and hoof picks in the tack room. She'd buy him new brushes soon—ones that had never been used by another horse before.

Natalie slipped the band of a currycomb over her hand and got to work. She started at the top of Tango's neck, moving the curry in small counterclockwise circles to loosen any dirt and shedding fur.

She heard footsteps coming down the aisle and looked up to see Marco Cruz, the fourteen-year-old boy who lived nearby and sometimes helped her dad with the ranch work after school.

"Hey, Natalie, who's this dapper hombre?" Marco asked. He was carrying a fifty-pound bag of fertilizer over one shoulder, but he paused to look at Tango without seeming to notice its weight.

A shock of dark-brown hair had fallen across one of his brown eyes, which always seemed filled with laughter. The way he tossed his head to flip back his bangs reminded Natalie of a proud horse showing off. Or of a silly boy in a pop band—she couldn't decide which.

According to her dad, Marco was a hard worker and a big help on the ranch. His only fault was that he teased Natalie and her sisters about everything, worse than an older brother.

To tell the truth, Natalie had a tiny, microscopic, barely measurable crush on Marco. But she'd go to school dressed as a rodeo clown before she let him know it. The only person she'd ever told was Sophia. Definitely not any of her sisters—especially Grace. She'd never hear the end of it.

"This is Tango, my new horse," said Natalie. She blushed a little as she said it, because she hadn't actually asked her parents if she could have him yet. But she was sure they wouldn't have a problem with her keeping Tango once they knew what a special bond the two of them already had.

"Oh yeah? Whatcha going to do with him?" asked

Marco, setting down the bag for a moment and wiping his brow with one tanned arm.

"Barrel racing, of course." Natalie ducked under Tango's neck and began to curry his other side.

"He trained for that?" asked Marco, looking Tango up and down.

"I'm not sure," said Natalie. "I haven't ridden him yet. But even if he isn't, he's so smart, I know he'll learn quickly."

Marco grinned. "I'd better watch out. You might get bored with barrel racing and become a regular rodeo queen. Next thing I know, you'll be taking home all the cutting and roping prizes, and I'll have to ride Pandora home empty-handed, with my hat down low to hide my face." He tilted his battered cowboy hat over his brow and slumped his shoulders in mock shame.

Natalie couldn't help laughing as she kept grooming Tango. Tango stood quietly, seeming to enjoy the attention. "Don't worry. The cattle of Texas are safe from my lariat for now," she said. "I've practiced roping barrels a little, and I managed to catch Grace once. But it'll be a while before I can rope and tie a calf in ten seconds flat."

Mr. Ramirez called Marco's name from somewhere outside. Marco heaved the bag of fertilizer over his shoulder once more and strolled down the aisle. "Adios for now, but I'll be sure to stop by again soon to see the wonder horse in action," he called over his free shoulder.

Natalie had finished currying Tango. Next, she used a dandy brush to sweep away the loosened hair and dirt. She followed that with a soft body brush to bring a shine to Tango's multicolored fur, once again working her way from the crest of his neck to the base of his tail.

Natalie took a metal hoof-pick from the grooming bucket and held it in her right hand while she leaned against Tango's shoulder, facing his tail. She ran her hand slowly down his leg and squeezed a spot midway down his cannon bone, clucking her tongue.

Tango immediately lifted his hoof and held it up while Natalie cupped her hand beneath it. She used the point of the pick to clean the dirt out of the grooves around the edges of the spongy, triangle-shaped frog that was the horse's natural shock absorber.

After she'd finished cleaning out all four of his hooves, she patted and praised him. "Someone taught you good manners, buddy," she said. A lot of horses didn't like having their feet handled and would try to pull their legs away—or even kick out. But Tango had been a perfect gentleman.

Because it was Tango's special welcome grooming, Natalie coated his hooves with clear polish, like she would for a show. Then she took a comb and worked all the tangles out of his black-and-white mane. It was black where his brown patches met the top of his neck, and white where his fur was white. His tail was all black, and she brushed it until it was as soft as a raven-colored cloud.

"Hey, Natalie, is everything okay in here?" called Emily from the doorway. She and Grace were leading their ponies back into the barn.

"Sure, why wouldn't it be?" asked Natalie. "And how come you're done riding so soon?"

"So soon?" asked Grace, looking puzzled. "It's almost six. We figured you decided not to ride after all."

"I told Grace we should only stay on the ponies for a half hour," said Emily. "But when you didn't come out, we decided to set up some cavalletti, and we sort of lost track of time."

Natalie glanced up at the clock above the tack room door. She was shocked to see that she had, indeed, been fussing over Tango for more than an hour. With a sinking feeling, Natalie took her phone out of her back pocket and saw that she had missed a FaceTime call from Sophia.

Just then, the girls' mother came into the barn. "There you all are!" she said. "What are you still doing outside? Grace and Emily, you know that study time starts at five sharp. And I've never known any of you to be late for pizza night before."

"Pizza night!" Grace squealed. "I totally forgot.

Oh no, and Abby can put away, like, six slices. I hope there's still some left for us."

"Be sure to take care of Joker and Bluebonnet before you come inside," said Mrs. Ramirez, pausing to pat each of the ponies. "And try to keep better track of time, okay? I spend enough of my day herding cats to be rounding up my children too!"

"It was my fault," Natalie said quickly. "I got so wrapped up grooming Tango that I didn't notice how late it was getting." She quickly put Tango into his stall and helped Emily and Grace untack their ponies.

I'm so sorry! she texted Sophia on her way into the house. *I was in the barn, and I lost track of time. Can we talk tomorrow instead?*

Sophia replied quickly: *Haha, typical Natalie ;) No problemo, ttyl!*

Natalie was relieved. She'd have known it if Sophia was mad.

Later that evening, Natalie updated the Second Chance Ranch blog with one of the pictures of Tango she'd taken in the pasture. She didn't have time to write much, so she just said that he was the ranch's newest resident and was settling in well but wasn't up for adoption yet.

And won't ever be, Natalie added to herself. Soon, she'd talk to her parents and tell them that she wanted Tango to be hers.

Chapter Four

"I pick Darcy."

Natalie gritted her teeth as Danica called Darcy over to her side of the basketball court. She was sure Danica was only being friendly because she had seen Natalie and Darcy having lunch together the day before—and because she knew Natalie had been planning to choose Darcy for her own team. Natalie called Owen Anderson over instead, because he was the tallest kid in seventh grade.

Her team ended up annihilating Danica's, with a score of 12–2 by the end of gym class. Darcy was a terrible basketball player; she cringed whenever someone threw the ball in her direction. But Natalie was still annoyed that Danica had made Darcy and Natalie play on opposite teams.

And now Danica and Riley were acting all friendly toward Darcy, complimenting her hair and outfit like they really cared. They were so two-faced. Earlier, Natalie had overheard Danica making fun of Darcy's pink glasses, and Riley had laughed right along with her.

"Riley and Danica don't seem so bad to me," Darcy said later, as she and Natalie ate lunch together. Even Darcy's lunches were fashionable. She had brought hers from home that day in a cute wooden tray with square compartments, each filled with a different food: cut-up kiwi, mango, cucumber, cheddar cheese, and white cubes that Darcy said were marinated tofu.

"Help yourself," she said, sliding the tray toward Natalie.

"Thanks." Natalie avoided the tofu but took a couple slices of kiwi, which was her favorite. She tried to think of a way to warn Darcy about Danica and Riley that wouldn't be adding more fuel to the bonfire of gossip that always crackled around those two. She couldn't do it, so she didn't say anything. If Darcy was as smart as she seemed, she'd figure them out quickly enough.

"I was thinking maybe you could come over and see the ranch this weekend, if you're not busy," said Natalie.

"I'd love to!" said Darcy. "I'm going to the movies with my mom on Saturday, but I'm free on Sunday afternoon."

"Great!" said Natalie. "What movie are you seeing?"

"*La Vie Souffre*," said Darcy dramatically, rolling the "r."

"Never heard of it," said Natalie. She hadn't seen it advertised when her family had gone to the movies a couple of weekends ago.

"It's a French art-house film with subtitles," said

Darcy. "That's why we're taking a day trip to Houston to see it. Sugarberry doesn't have an independent theater."

"Yeah, it's not really that kind of town," Natalie remarked. Downtown Sugarberry was pretty basic, but she liked it. And she'd always found plenty to watch at the regular old Saguaro Cineplex. She felt bad that Darcy had to drive such a long way to see such a boring-sounding movie. But Darcy sounded cheerful about it.

"Anyway, if you're going to Houston, you should definitely check out Sam's Spice Kitchen. Best Tex-Mex food in the city."

"Cool, but my mom and I always get sushi after we go to a movie. It's kind of our thing."

Natalie shuddered a little. She couldn't imagine anyone eating chunks of raw fish because they *wanted* to—and not because they were shipwrecked or something. But maybe it was something Darcy had eaten since she was a little kid, the way Natalie loved mole sauce even though most of her non-Mexican friends thought it was weird. Except, Natalie was pretty sure sushi was Japanese, and Darcy had said her family was Chinese-American.

Anyway, Natalie was just glad she had invited Darcy over before Danica and Riley could con her into going shoplifting at the mall or whatever it was they did on weekends. Darcy had already proven that she was a good friend. That morning, outside the classroom before their quiz, she'd been all ready to give Natalie a crash course on the plot of *Holes*. Natalie had managed to skim the book the night before—before she'd fallen asleep—but she thought it was sweet that Darcy had offered.

After lunch, the girls headed off to science lab, where Natalie steered Darcy away from the stinky sulfur corner. Unfortunately, Mr. Vincent always assigned lab partners, and Natalie and Darcy ended up in different groups. They didn't get a chance to talk again for the rest of the day. She only had time to give Darcy a quick wave in the parking lot before they got on different school buses. Except, instead of just doing a normal wave, Darcy made an over-the-top movement with her whole arm and clutched at her heart while dancing backward on tiptoes. Natalie burst into laughter. She was really looking forward to spending time with Darcy that weekend.

But on the bus ride home, as she stared out at the passing cattle ranches and open fields blooming with Indian paintbrush and other wildflowers, Natalie began to second-guess herself.

As far as she was concerned, loyalty was one of the most important things in life. Her father was the one who had taught her what it meant. When she was a little kid—so young that Abby didn't remember, and Emily and Grace hadn't even joined the family

yet—her dad had been in the army. Sometimes, he'd be away for months at a time. Natalie had gotten angry once and asked why he left her for so long, if he loved her as much as he said he did.

She'd never forgotten his answer: He'd said that loyalty meant doing what was best for the people and things you cared most about—your family, your friends, and your country—even if it was really hard sometimes.

If Natalie started doing all the fun things with Darcy that she used to do with Sophia, what kind of friend was she being?

Not a best friend, that was for sure. Maybe not even a friend at all.

"Whoa, Tango. Good boy." Natalie halted Tango next to the wooden mounting block. She slid her left foot into the wide stirrup of the Western saddle, then swung her right leg over Tango's back and tried to clear her mind of all her worries as she settled into the saddle's deep, comfortable seat.

Natalie held the reins in her right hand and squeezed gently with her heels. Tango's ears flicked back with uncertainty for a moment. His neck stiffened.

"Walk on," said Natalie. She squeezed slightly harder and gave an encouraging cluck. Tango relaxed and stepped forward into a smooth, alert walk.

"How does he feel?" asked Grace.

"She's only been on him for three strides, silly," said Emily.

The girls were sitting on the arena fence, watching Natalie ride. Mr. Ramirez was nearby, doing some yard work, but he paused from time to time to look over at the arena. The audience made Natalie feel a little nervous.

"So far, so good," said Natalie. She made two circles of the sandy arena before changing direction

across the diagonal line. At first, Tango didn't seem to notice when she asked him to turn, just like he had ignored her signal to walk. But finally, he got the message and moved off the rail.

After a couple of circles in the other direction, Natalie asked Tango to jog. He moved willingly into the gait, but he was going too fast. Natalie felt herself bouncing in the saddle. She leaned back slightly and drew back on the reins to slow him. Tango halted, and Natalie was thrown forward against the saddle horn.

Natalie took a few deep breaths, knowing it wasn't fair to take her frustration out on Tango. He wasn't being bad, exactly. He just didn't seem to understand quite what she was asking.

Wondering exactly what would happen, Natalie slid her outside leg back and asked Tango to lope. He sprang into the gait at once, and she let out a sigh of relief. He was still going too fast, but his strides were as smooth as glass.

"Should we set up some barrels?" asked Grace.

"I think that's enough for today," said Natalie quickly, asking Tango to walk. Once again, he halted abruptly. But she was prepared for it, sort of.

"You've hardly done anything yet!" said Grace. "But if you're finished riding already, can I try him out?"

Natalie hesitated. "I guess so," she said. It wasn't

like Tango was bucking or misbehaving. She was pretty sure he'd be safe for her sister to ride.

"Remember that he's in Western tack, so you'll be neck reining instead of using direct rein signal," she said as she shortened the stirrups and boosted her sister into the saddle. The girls rode hunt seat, so they were used to English tack and commands. "Lay the reins on his neck toward whatever direction you want him to go."

"I know how to neck rein," said Grace, nudging Tango into a walk, then a jog.

With Grace riding, Tango's confusion was even clearer. He zigzagged down the straightaways and drifted like a ship at sea when Grace asked him to turn.

"Wow, he's really green," said Grace, halting after a few minutes. "I wonder if he's even been trained."

"He's got to be," said Emily. "Mom looked at his teeth, and she said he's around seven or eight years old. Most horses are trained by two or three."

"Not always," Grace shot back. "How many times have we rescued older horses who've been sitting around in a pasture for their whole lives? Or maybe he was trained once, but he hasn't been ridden in so long that he forgot."

Grace dismounted, gave Tango a quick pat, and handed the reins to Natalie. As she led him back to the barn, Natalie found herself thinking up possible excuses for Tango's less-than-stellar performance. Maybe he was still getting used to the farm and was distracted by all the new sights and smells. Or maybe it was like Grace said, and he was only green-broke. Lots of horses were ridden a few times by a professional horsebreaker before they went somewhere like a summer camp or a trail-riding stable for tourists. They learned to more or less stop and go on command, but they were never taught the finer points of leg and rein signals.

If that was the case, Natalie could work with Tango, and eventually, he might become as responsive as Rockette had been. Natalie gave Tango a carrot, smiling as he took it politely from her outstretched palm. At the end of the day, a horse's attitude was more important than anything, and she could sense Tango's sweetness.

Natalie's phone timer buzzed in her pocket. She'd set it that morning, and now she silenced it without looking. She already knew it was her reminder to call Sophia.

Chapter Five

"Hola, chica!" Sophia's cheerful voice sounded over the phone a couple of seconds before the video stream buffered and brought her image to life.

"Hey! How's life on the East Coast?" said Natalie.

"Freezing. April isn't really spring here—we had six inches of snow last week!"

Looking at her friend's familiar face on the small screen, a lot of Natalie's anxiety vanished. No matter how much time had passed since she'd talked to Sophia, it always seemed like they picked up right where they'd left off.

"Did you see the new episode of *Zombie Academy*?" asked Natalie. It was their favorite show.

"Do I look dead?" said Sophia. "Because you *know* that's the only way I would miss it."

"Can you believe that Jeb gave Harper the last dose of antidote right before the zombie prom?"

"I know, right?" said Sophia. "I cried—I'm not ashamed to admit it."

They spent another fifteen minutes analyzing the episode. Natalie sat cross-legged on her bed, stroking Autumn while they talked. She could see Sophia's new room in the background, set up almost exactly like

her old one had been, down to the poster of Jackson Xavier, star of *Zombie Academy*, above her bed.

"How's your dad's new job going?" asked Natalie. It was the reason Sophia's family had moved.

Sophia made a "so-so" face. "He has to work longer hours than he used to, and he complains about the commute on the T a lot," she said. "That's the subway here. There's so much traffic that hardly anyone drives. Listen, you can hear it in the background."

Natalie listened. She could hear the dull roar of passing cars and the sound of a siren in the distance.

"But I guess he likes the job okay," Sophia added. "It pays better than his old one. He took us all to the

Boston Aquarium last weekend and then to a really great restaurant on the harbor."

"Well, maybe he'll decide that he liked Texas better and move back here," said Natalie hopefully. "Not much traffic in Sugarberry."

Every time they'd talked since Sophia moved away, they'd come up with elaborate plans to get her back to Texas, where she belonged. Sophia had even asked if she could be a working student at Second Chance Ranch. But both sets of parents had agreed she wasn't old enough for that.

"Maybe," said Sophia, but she didn't sound very hopeful. "How's everything at the ranch? I saw on the blog that Cocoa had her puppies. And who's this new horse? Your post didn't say much about him."

Natalie was a little surprised that Sophia had dropped the subject of her finding a way back home so quickly. But right then, she was too excited to tell Sophia about Tango to worry about it.

"Oh, he's amazing, Soph." Natalie thought about her ride that afternoon. "Or at least, he will be. He still needs some training." She told Sophia about the Paint's unknown past and her plans to turn him into a barrel-racing star.

"That's awesome!" said Sophia. "I'm so glad you finally found another horse as cool as Rockette."

Natalie grinned. She knew Sophia would understand.

"You'll have to take more pictures soon," said Sophia. "Or even better, a video."

"I will," Natalie promised. *Once Tango's made a tiny bit more progress*, she added to herself.

"I'll have to show the video to Olivia and Brie," Sophia went on. "Neither of them have ridden a horse before. Can you believe it? They'd be blown away by a video of you on a barrel-racing course."

"Who are Olivia and Brie?" asked Natalie.

"My friends from school," said Sophia. "Didn't I mention them before?"

"No, I don't think so," said Natalie. "But I guess we haven't talked in a while."

"I wish you could meet them," said Sophia. "But you will when you come to visit, of course. Maybe over summer vacation."

"I thought you were planning to come *here* for summer vacation," said Natalie with a frown.

"Yeah, we'll see," said Sophia vaguely. "Maybe we can do both! How fab would that be? Anyway, I think you'd really like them. Brie has this totally sarcastic sense of humor you'd appreciate. And Olivia trained her betta fish to do tricks. Can you believe it?"

Natalie couldn't—not that Olivia had trained her fish, but that Sophia thought Natalie would care. As she listened to Sophia chattering on about all the "epically hilarious" things her new friends had said and done, a white-hot feeling rose up in Natalie's chest.

"Listen, I've got to go help my mom with a sick cat," she said, cutting Sophia off in the middle of a story about the three girls getting lost in the Boston Common.

"Oh, okay," said Sophia, sounding disappointed. "Talk again soon?"

"Um, yeah, sure," said Natalie. She quickly ended the call.

There was no sick cat, of course. Natalie had just lied to her best friend. Except it seemed like Sophia already had a *new* best friend. Two of them, actually, which wasn't even supposed to be possible.

Or maybe Sophia had never been what Natalie had thought she was. It was one thing for Sophia to hang out with kids at her new school, but it was like she'd totally given up on the idea of moving back to Texas. She didn't even sound that eager to visit.

And if that was true, Natalie was free to have as much fun with Darcy as she wanted. Maybe Darcy would make a more loyal best friend than Sophia had ended up being.

Natalie had been planning to ride Tango in the arena after school the next afternoon, but Emily and Grace convinced her to join them on a trail ride instead.

The path they took cut across the fenced-in pasture of a nearby cattle ranch. Emily, whose pony, Bluebonnet, was the calmest, reached down and opened the gate while the others filed through. She then closed it behind her.

While they were crossing the pasture, a curious calf broke away from the herd and trotted toward them. Tango stopped dead in his tracks, his muscles bunched up. He snorted through flared nostrils, and his whole body trembled. Natalie closed her leg, tightened up on the reins, and said his name to get his attention.

But Tango didn't even seem to notice. As the calf came closer, Tango spun around and bolted in the other direction. Natalie could barely hang on tight enough to avoid being dumped on the rocky ground.

She managed to stop Tango just before they crashed into a string of barbed-wire fence. "Easy, easy . . ." she said, her voice shaking slightly.

Emily came trotting over on Bluebonnet, while Grace and Joker drove the calf back to the herd.

"Are you okay?" called Emily.

"I think so," said Natalie, her heart still pounding. Tango stuck to Bluebonnet's side like a burr as they crossed the pasture again. He was acting like he'd never seen a cow before. But for a horse living in Texas ranch country, that seemed nearly impossible.

By the time they got back to the barn, Tango's

coat was lathered with sweat. It was a warm day, so Natalie decided to give him a bath. She asked Emily and Grace to give her a hand, in case Tango was as nervous about water as he was about cattle.

But to her surprise, he stood quietly in the concrete wash stall while they hosed him off and lathered him with horse shampoo.

Natalie set the running hose on the ground for a moment while she searched for a squeegee to help rinse off the suds. She felt a cold spray hit her back.

"Grace!" she shrieked. "I'm going to—" She whirled around to see Tango holding the hose in his mouth, bobbing his head up and down while the water gushed from the hose. He looked like a horse-shaped fountain. The whole back of Natalie's shirt was soaked through. Nearby, Emily and Grace were practically rolling on the ground with laughter.

Natalie couldn't help laughing too. She reclaimed the hose and finished rinsing Tango off, then used the squeegee to whisk most of the water from his coat.

His fur was still damp, so she led him onto the lawn to graze in the sun. The grass there was lusher and more tender than the grass in the pasture, and Tango cropped it eagerly. As his coat dried, his white patches shone a pure snowy color, and his brown patches glistened like copper. He really was one of the most beautiful horses Natalie had ever seen.

That night at dinner, Natalie's father said that the owner of a girls' boarding school in North Texas had called, asking if the ranch had two sound, reliable horses available for adoption.

"They've got great references," he added. "And a beautiful facility. I was thinking we might offer them Dolly and maybe that new Paint, as well, since he seems to be good-tempered and safe with children. What do you think, Natalie?"

She nearly choked on a bite of baked potato. It was now or never.

"Actually," she said, "I was thinking I might like to keep Tango for myself." She crossed her fingers under the table.

"Really?" said her father, looking surprised. "I thought you were hoping to find a new barrel horse. He's not trained for that, is he?"

"Well, no," Natalie admitted. "But he's really smart, so I'm sure he can learn."

Natalie's parents exchanged thoughtful glances.

"If you're sure you'd like to keep him, I have no problem with that," said her mother. "But wouldn't you rather keep looking for a more experienced horse? I know you were looking forward to competing this summer."

"That's okay," said Natalie. "I'm sure that Tango's the one for me."

"In that case, he's all yours," said Natalie's father. "I'll think of another horse to offer to the school."

Natalie breathed a sigh of relief. Even the worries left over from her conversation with Sophia seemed to fade in the glow of her excitement. How could she be upset about anything when she had a horse of her own again?

Chapter Six

The next day was Saturday, and Natalie was so busy helping with the ranch's open house that she didn't have time to give Tango more than a quick grooming. She ended up helping Abby in the kennel while Mr. Ramirez and Grace talked to people interested in the horses and ponies, and Mrs. Ramirez and Emily showed people the cats and other animals.

Amigo sat near the kennel doorway, offering visitors his paw to shake as they entered. Abby had taught him that trick herself. Normally, a service dog was supposed to pay attention only to its owner and not be handled by other people. But now that Amigo was semi-retired and off duty, he loved being the ranch's ambassador.

An elderly man came in and asked about the puppies he'd seen online. Natalie showed him to Cocoa and her litter in their pen.

"That one looks just like my old dog," he said, his eyes lighting up. He pointed at Clove, who was flopped down on the floor next to Abby, chewing a rope toy. "Yes, he'll be perfect."

Abby seemed to take in the man's cane. "What kind of house do you live in?" she asked.

"Oh, I live in Sunset Ridge Senior Apartments," he said.

"Tell me about your old dog," said Abby, twirling her short light-brown hair around her finger.

"Winston? Oh, he was wonderful. Faithful as can be and never more than a few steps from my side. Loved sitting on the couch and watching old movies, and he wouldn't take his eyes off the screen."

"Hmm," said Abby. "Your apartment, does it have a big yard?"

"None at all," said the man. "I live on the third floor. Just as well—I'm getting a bit stiff in the knees to be keeping a lawn mowed and tidy. Anyway, how much should I make out a check for, to put a deposit on this little fellow?"

"You can donate any amount you'd like," said Abby, "but you can't put a deposit on this puppy."

Natalie looked at Abby in surprise. The man sounded like he would probably be a great owner. Sure, it would have been nice if he had a yard, but was that really important? Lots of dogs lived in apartments.

The man looked surprised too. "Is he already spoken for? The woman I talked to outside said all six puppies were available."

"They are but only to the right owners," said Abby. "Clove might *look* like your old dog, but he's very independent and active. He wouldn't like living in an apartment, and he would probably chew on the furniture."

"Is that so?" said the man, frowning down at the black puppy, who was still busily gnawing on the rope toy.

"But we have another puppy that would be perfect for you." Abby picked up Cinnamon. "She's very social, but she doesn't have a lot of energy like Clove, so she won't mind living mostly indoors."

"I don't know . . ." The man looked from Clove to Cinnamon and back again. Clove had gotten tired of the rope toy and was trying to climb out of the pen again. Cinnamon lay contentedly in Abby's arms and turned her head to lick her elbow.

Abby held out Cinnamon. The man hesitated for

a moment, set his cane against the pen, and took the puppy. She licked *his* elbow too. "Well now, I suppose this one might do," he said gruffly, stroking the puppy's soft brown head.

While Abby and Natalie had been helping the man choose a puppy, several more people had come into the kennel to meet the dogs that were available for adoption. One of them was a young woman who loved hiking and trail running. It turned out that Clove met his match that day, after all.

By the end of the open house, Natalie was exhausted but happy. Along with Cinnamon and Clove, Ashes the cat and Veronica the goat had found new homes. The ranch had also gotten more than $800 in adoption fees and donations.

Later, as she updated the Second Chance Ranch blog to tell people about the animals that had been adopted, a chat request from Sophia popped up. Natalie felt a little guilty as she set her status to "busy" and didn't reply. But it wasn't like she was ignoring Sophia—she really did have lots to do.

Sophia had her new life in Boston, and Natalie was starting a new chapter of her old life in Texas. It wasn't like Natalie needed to hear every detail of whatever new trick Olivia had taught her betta fish or whatever "epically hilarious" thing Brie had said. Just like Sophia didn't need to know that Natalie was planning to spend the afternoon with Darcy tomorrow.

But they'd talk again eventually. They were still friends, after all.

Just maybe not best friends anymore.

Chapter Seven

Around noon the next day, a blue Volvo pulled into the driveway. Darcy hopped out, and Natalie hurried across the yard to greet her. Today Darcy was wearing a black sundress with zebra-print leggings underneath and black lace-up wedges.

A dark-haired woman waved at Natalie from the driver's seat. "Nice to meet you," she said. "I'm Susan." She wore glasses like Darcy, but the frames of hers were emerald green.

"Nice to meet you, too," said Natalie. "Would you like to come inside for a little while?"

"Thank you, but I'm off to lunch with a friend," she said. "You girls have fun!"

"How was that movie, *La Vie Soufflé*?" Natalie asked Darcy as they headed for the house.

"*La Vie* Souffre," said Darcy with a giggle. "It means 'Life Is Suffering.' And it was so sad . . . I cried for nearly the whole three hours."

"I'm sorry," said Natalie.

"No, it was amazing," said Darcy. "And it was a really fun day overall. My mom and I ate tons of sashimi and udon noodles for lunch, and then we went shopping in downtown Houston. That's where I got these leggings. What do you think of them?"

"They're really . . . vivid," said Natalie, trying to be tactful without actually lying.

"I thought they were double-underline cool when I saw them on the mannequin, but now I'm not so sure," said Darcy. "Don't you hate it when you try on an outfit in the store and it looks perfect, and then you wear it at home and realize it's not working at all?"

"Yeah, totally," said Natalie. The truth was that she went to the mall about twice a year, bought enough jeans, sweatshirts, and T-shirts to last for the semester, and then got out as fast as she could.

"Wow, what a cool place!" said Darcy, looking around with obvious delight at the yard, the barn, and the acres of fenced pasture.

"Thanks," said Natalie, pleased that Darcy liked the ranch. "I'd introduce you to my family, but they all went to watch Grace's soccer game this afternoon. So you'll just have to settle for meeting the animals for now."

Natalie brought Darcy to the kennel. She squealed with delight when she saw Cocoa's puppies. Natalie picked up a wriggling Ginger and started to hand him to Darcy.

"Oh, I can't," said Darcy, looking like she was trying hard to resist. "I love dogs, but I'm really allergic. Cats too. I took some medicine before I came, so I'm fine being in the same room with them. But I can't really handle them, or I could have an asthma attack."

"I thought you had a cat," said Natalie.

"She's a sphynx," said Darcy, as if that were an explanation. She added, "It's hairless, so it's considered hypoallergenic."

"Oh," said Natalie, setting Ginger back down, where he began to play tug-of-war with her shoelaces.

Darcy asked a lot of questions about the dogs, and then she and Natalie moved on to the cattery. Darcy talked to all the cats in a funny, squeaky voice, and even the shyest ones approached and rubbed against her legs.

"Is that okay?" asked Natalie, a little worried that Darcy would suddenly stop breathing or something.

"It's fine," said Darcy, beaming down at the purring Autumn. "I'll just put these leggings in the washing machine when I get home."

Darcy couldn't pick up the rabbits, either, but she did hold Cadbury's leash while they took the big Holland lop out for a walk—or rather, a *hop*—around the yard. Afterward, they walked out to the horse pasture. Natalie climbed over the fence and started walking over to the herd.

Tango looked up at her and whinnied. Once again, he was standing apart from the herd on the grassy edge of the ridge, which was higher than the rest of the property. It made him look like a statue on a pedestal against the perfect blue sky.

Halfway across the pasture, when Natalie glanced

back, she saw that Darcy was still sitting on the fence. "You can come into the pasture!" she called.

"Oh, no thanks!" Darcy yelled back. "The horses are beautiful, but I think I'll just watch them from here."

Natalie had been planning to show off Tango to Darcy and even let her ride him if she wanted. But it sounded like that wasn't going to work. She tried to think what else they could do. "Do you want to get something to eat and watch a movie?" she suggested, returning to the fence.

"Sure," said Darcy, her attention still on the horses. She laughed as little Joker drove Dolly, the huge half draft mare, away from a tasty patch of clover that he wanted for himself.

When they got back to the kitchen, Darcy admired

the pottery on the counter and Emily's drawings on the refrigerator door.

"What would you like to drink?" asked Natalie, opening the fridge. "Looks like we've got orange juice, ginger ale, and horchata."

"What's that last one?" asked Darcy.

"It's a Mexican drink made with rice and cinnamon."

"That sounds yummy," said Darcy.

Natalie poured a big glass. Then she got out tortilla chips, shredded cheese, salsa, chili peppers, green olives, red-pepper flakes, and an unlabeled bottle of bright-red sauce.

"What are you making?" asked Darcy, sipping her horchata. "Mmm, this *is* good."

"My friend Sophia and I always made this as a snack when she came over," said Natalie. "Quadruple-alarm nachos!"

"Why are they 'alarmed'?" asked Darcy warily. "Are they extremely spicy? Because I don't really like extremely spicy food."

"My sister Emily doesn't either, and even she can't resist the deliciosity of these nachos," said Natalie. "They're called quadruple-alarm because they have four different kinds of zing: chili peppers, homemade hot sauce, red-pepper flakes, and salsa."

Darcy gulped. Natalie proceeded to chop, shred, and pile ingredients onto a plate of tortilla chips, then stuck the whole concoction in the microwave. A minute later, she pulled out a plate of molten cheesy chips filled with hot-sauce lava pools and studded with bright bits of salsa and pepper.

"If you're worried about the heat, a little sour cream really takes it down a notch." Natalie grabbed the container from the fridge and dolloped a few spoonfuls over the nachos. She slid the loaded plate across the counter toward Darcy. "Don't be shy! Dig in!"

Darcy took a chip from the very edge of the plate—with barely any cheese or sauce on it. She took a cautious nibble and then quickly swallowed a big gulp of horchata.

"Mmm," she said unconvincingly.

Well, that was okay. Not everyone shared Natalie's love for fiery food. "Hey, do you want to watch an episode of *Zombie High*?" she asked as they headed into the den. "I've got the first three seasons on DVD."

"Is it really a show about zombies who go to high school?" asked Darcy.

"Yup. It's awesome," said Natalie.

"Um . . ." Darcy glanced at the shelf filled with movies next to the TV. "Hey, is that *Amélie*? It's my favorite! Do you want to watch it?"

Natalie had never seen that movie before. She'd really been looking forward to getting Darcy hooked on *Zombie High*—but Darcy was the guest, so it was only polite to watch what she wanted.

"Sure," said Natalie, popping the disc into the DVD player. *Amélie* ended up being a long, confusing French film with subtitles. Darcy seemed to have a thing for those. Natalie fidgeted in her seat for the entire movie. She looked out the window at the horses playing in the pasture. She coaxed Autumn off her seat in the windowsill and entertained her with a feather toy on a string until Autumn got bored and fell back asleep. Natalie wished she could do the same. But Darcy seemed entranced, her eyes glued to the screen.

Just as the movie was ending, Natalie saw Ms. Chang's car pull into the driveway. "Looks like your mom's here," she said.

"Oh, too bad," said Darcy. "I was having so much fun! Thanks for inviting me over."

"Yeah, thanks for coming." Natalie walked Darcy out to the car and waved while she watched her drive away.

When she was gone, Natalie breathed a sigh of relief. Darcy had seemed like so much fun at school. But what was Natalie supposed to do with a friend that was allergic to dogs and cats, scared of horses, hated Natalie's favorite foods, and liked weird movies that didn't make any sense?

Natalie thought of all the fun afternoons she and

Sophia had spent together. If Sophia had visited to-day, they probably would have played with Cocoa's puppies, given some of the other dogs a bath, taken a trail ride, dared each other to reach new levels of hot-sauce intensity, and binge-watched *Zombie High* until Natalie's mom made them turn off the TV.

But Darcy wasn't anything like Sophia, and Natalie was starting to think they didn't have much in common after all.

Chapter Eight

At least there was still time for Natalie to ride that afternoon. She might as well start practicing her barrel pattern on Tango.

She went out to the arena and set up three large, empty oil drums in a triangle pattern. The rules of barrel racing were simple. First, the rider entered the arena at a gallop, then she could circle either the near left-hand or right-hand barrel first. Whichever she chose, her horse would make a circle to the right around that barrel.

Then horse and rider moved on to the second barrel and circled it to the left. The third barrel, at the end of the arena, was also circled to the left. After that was a mad gallop down the straightaway to the finish line.

If the horse knocked down any of the barrels, the pair got a five-second penalty. That didn't sound like much, but it was *huge* in barrel racing. It took a lot of practice to know how close to cut the turns and how much to rate the horse's speed around the barrels. Natalie had put in that practice. She was pretty good, and she wanted to get better.

Rockette had been one fast pony, perfect for the under-twelve rodeo divisions. But her legs had been just too short to outpace older riders on full-sized horses. A big, athletic horse like Tango, though, could have what it took to go all the way to the top—or, at least, all the way to the Under-Eighteen State Championships, which was Natalie's dream. If by some miracle she won the title this summer, she'd be the youngest rider ever to do it.

And it probably will *take a miracle*, Natalie reminded herself. It didn't seem likely that Tango would be any more familiar with barrels than he was with cattle. She hoped he'd at least find the barrels less terrifying.

Natalie tacked him up quickly and led him out to the arena. She wasn't supposed to ride alone, but she could see Marco in the yard nearby, stringing up some new fencing around the ranch's chicken coop. Natalie figured that was close enough to someone watching.

She warmed Tango up by walking, jogging, and loping around the arena.

Then she turned him toward the barrels and steered him around the cloverleaf pattern at a walk. So far, so good.

Next, she tried a jog. Tango's circles were a bit wide. It felt like there was a delay between when she asked him to turn and when he responded. Natalie didn't know what to make of it. She tried the pattern again at a lope, and this time their circles were so big that Tango drifted nearly out to the rail before finally getting the message to turn.

Natalie groaned as she saw Marco leave the chicken coop and head over to the arena. He put one boot up on the lowest rail of the gate and folded his arms across the top. "Looks like that outlaw's givin' you some trouble," he said, exaggerating his natural Texas drawl like he did when he thought he was being clever.

Natalie didn't respond. She just urged Tango into a lope and headed for the barrels again. She'd show Marco. She leaned forward and clucked her tongue to quicken Tango's pace to a gallop.

She sat up as they approached the barrel and asked Tango to turn earlier than she had before. She leaned hard to the left, throwing her weight into the left stirrup as she leaned the right rein firmly on Tango's neck.

Tango responded immediately this time. The problem was, Natalie had been expecting him to hesitate, so she'd asked too soon. Instead of circling the barrel, Tango crashed into it hard with his shoulder.

The barrel smacked against Natalie's leg and then went flying. Tango stumbled and fell to his knees. Natalie saw flashes of the house beyond, Marco climbing over the gate, and the sandy floor of the arena all mixed-up as she flew over Tango's head.

She landed with a *thud* that knocked the breath

out of her. Then she heard the sound of galloping hoofbeats—or was that her own pulse thundering in her ears? Her vision swam with flashes of light.

The next thing she knew, Marco was by her side, his deep-brown eyes staring down at her with concern. "You okay?" he said, helping her sit up. "That was a pretty rough spill."

"I'm fine." Natalie stood up, her cheeks blazing with embarrassment. She brushed the dirt off her clothes as best she could, straightened her helmet, and looked around the arena to find Tango standing in the corner, hanging his head.

She walked over to him with her hand outstretched and picked up his trailing reins. "Sorry, buddy, that was my fault," she said, patting his neck.

"Set up that barrel again for me, will you?" she called to Marco.

He did as she asked. Natalie thought he looked like he wanted to say something but was holding his tongue, which was pretty weird behavior for Marco.

Natalie remounted and rode around the arena for a few minutes until she felt Tango—and herself—relax. Then she took him around the barrels at a walk, followed by a jog. When they completed the pattern a second time, Natalie dismounted. Maybe she should have taken him through at a lope again, but she just didn't feel like it. Especially with Marco watching.

She half-expected him to make a teasing comment

as she led Tango past on the way back to the barn. But he didn't say a word. He just stood nearby, watching while she untacked Tango, and then he insisted on carrying the heavy Western saddle back to the tack room for her.

Natalie didn't say so, but she was grateful. Her whole body was stiff and sore from the fall. Nothing felt sprained or broken, but she knew she'd have a big bruise on her knee the next day where the barrel had hit it. Her confidence felt more bruised than her body, though.

Did Natalie really have what it took to turn Tango into a barrel-racing star? What if Tango wasn't as good as she thought? Or worse—what if *Natalie* wasn't?

Chapter Nine

At lunchtime on Monday, Darcy hurried over to sit with Natalie like she'd done all last week. They had fun talking and joking as usual and then went over a tough homework assignment for math class. Natalie had been totally confused, but Darcy managed to explain quadratic equations in a way that made sense, unlike Ms. Fiori's rambling lecture.

Thanks to Darcy, Natalie managed to fix her answers before class, which probably saved her from getting grounded from riding for a few days because of a bad grade.

Natalie started to wonder if maybe she'd been wrong about Darcy after all.

Then on Tuesday, Darcy asked if Natalie wanted to hang out with her that weekend. "I take a yoga class every Saturday morning, and I can bring a guest to the class for free," she said. "Do you want to go with me?"

"A yoga class?" Natalie echoed. She couldn't imagine herself in that pose that made people look like a bowing dog, or the one where people twisted up their legs like a pretzel.

"It's really fun," said Darcy. "You feel so relaxed by the end, but energized too."

Natalie still wasn't sure. But Darcy went on: "After the class, we can hang out at my house, and you can meet Cleopatra."

That sounded more like Natalie's idea of fun. "Okay," she agreed. "Do I have to wear leggings?" Natalie hated leggings. They made her legs feel like they were suffocating, and she thought they looked silly too.

"Only if you want to," said Darcy. "Jeans work, too, but they're not as good for flexibility."

Natalie was definitely not going to be trying any yoga positions that couldn't be done in her favorite pair of jeans. In fact, she didn't really feel like trying any yoga positions at all, especially when she could have gone to a rodeo instead.

But she had already agreed, so what could she do? Natalie sighed as Darcy started telling her about the difference between a sun salute and something called a tree pose . . .

When Natalie got home from school that afternoon, only Emily was in the stable. Abby had taken Amigo for a walk, and Mrs. Ramirez was still at work. Mr. Ramirez had gone to the feed store, and Grace had gone with him.

"She really wanted to get Joker a new halter with

neon-green reflective strips," Emily explained. "She saw them advertised in the store's newsletter."

Natalie helped Emily clean stalls, scrub water buckets, and sweep the barn aisle. Together, they went outside to refill the trough in the pasture.

Tango was galloping up and down along the pasture fence line, looking out toward the road and whinnying from time to time.

"I wonder what's got him so riled up," said Emily as he whizzed past without even looking at them.

Natalie grabbed his halter from the barn, figuring it would be a good idea to get him inside until he calmed down. She emerged just in time to see Tango gather himself up and leap effortlessly over the four-and-a-half-foot pasture fence.

For a second, Natalie couldn't believe her eyes. Then she saw Tango galloping down the driveway toward the road, and she knew that she had to act *now*.

"Quick, Emily! Grab Jaguar from the pasture!" she said, pushing the halter into her sister's hands. She ran into the barn and grabbed a set of tack and a lariat from the tack room.

When she returned, Emily was leading a lean bay quarter horse through the pasture gate. Jaguar was a retired champion roping horse—but he was coming out of retirement for a day!

Natalie quickly threw on Jaguar's saddle and bridle, tying the end of the lariat to the saddle horn.

Emily gave her a leg up onto his back. Natalie urged Jaguar into a fast lope as they followed in the direction that Tango had gone.

There wasn't much traffic on the winding country road in front of the ranch, but the cars that did go by were often speeding. Natalie hated to think what could happen if one of them met Tango on the road. She knew she was putting herself in a dangerous situation too. But what choice did she have?

The driveway was on the crest of a hill that offered a good view of the surrounding landscape. Natalie could see Tango zigzagging down the road ahead. On the horizon about a mile away, a red sports car zoomed down the narrow road like a car in a TV commercial, raising clouds of dust in its wake. It disappeared around a hairpin turn, but Natalie knew it was only a matter of time before the car crossed Tango's path.

She kicked Jaguar into a gallop. He was a quarter horse, built for fast sprints. Even though he was nearly twenty years old, his top speed took Natalie's breath away. Ahead of them, Tango was still veering from one side of the road to another.

Jaguar closed the gap between them with every stride, legs moving like pistons, hooves pounding on the road. Natalie twirled her lariat in the air, praying that her aim would be better than it had ever been when she'd roped barrels for practice.

As Jaguar drew up alongside Tango, Natalie let the lariat fly. She held her breath as the loop of rope fell over Tango's head and tightened around his neck. She sat back to slow Jaguar down, and Tango was forced to check his pace, too, as the rope grew taut.

Natalie managed to bring him back down to a jolting trot. She steered both horses off the road and into the underbrush just as the sports car rounded the bend. It came flying past at what had to have been eighty miles per hour, its radio blaring.

Tango tried to bolt, but Jaguar dug in his heels and held him fast, the rope straining between them. Natalie managed to get them both turned around and ponied Tango along the edge of the road back to the ranch.

Emily was waiting at the end of the driveway, clutching Tango's halter so tightly that her knuckles were white. "I was so scared when I saw that car coming," she said. "I didn't know you could rope like that!"

"Me neither," said Natalie with a shaky laugh. She slid off Jaguar's back. When she hit the ground, her legs felt like jelly. She took the halter from Emily and slipped it over Tango's head, lifting the lariat from around his neck as she did so. He had a mild rope burn where the lasso had cut into his neck.

"I'd better put some ointment on this," she said. Both horses also had scratches on their legs from the prickly sagebrush, but none looked deep.

"I'll look after Jaguar," said Emily, stepping forward and taking his reins. The quarter horse was breathing heavily, his fur darkened with sweat.

Natalie brought Tango into his stall and gave him some hay to distract him while she rinsed the rope burn on his neck with warm water and then dabbed it with antiseptic salve. She cleaned the smaller scrapes on his legs and then brushed the thorns and bits of broken twig out of his tail.

"Silly boy," she said, stepping forward toward his head. "What was all that for?" Tango looked around at the sound of her voice and let out a soft snort. But if that was an answer to Natalie's question, she didn't understand it.

She latched his stall and went to check on Jaguar. Emily had sponged off his coat and was picking out his hooves.

"He picked up a stone in the left fore, so he might have a bruise," she said. "But he's walking sound, so I think he'll be okay."

Natalie gave Jaguar two peppermints and a hug. If he had shown just a little less speed or obedience, she and Tango could both have been killed. "You were amazing, pal," she murmured.

"Let's leave him and Tango in their stalls for now," she said to Emily. "Mom should check them over when she gets home from work. Besides, if Tango jumped over that fence once, he could do it again."

"Yeah," said Emily. "It's weird. Usually, a horse would have to be really spooked to jump a fence that high. But he did it kind of effortlessly, did you see? He looked like one of the show jumpers at the Rolex Kentucky Event on TV."

It *was* weird. And more than a little worrying. Had Tango run away from his old home after jumping his fence? Would he do the same to Natalie one day? Even though Tango belonged to her now, something about him still felt mysterious and out of reach.

Chapter Ten

The next day, Natalie hardly said a word while Darcy talked about her ideas for a new fashion line based on the colors and patterns of sushi rolls.

Natalie went through the day on autopilot, counting the minutes until she could get out to the barn to work with Tango. He needed more of her attention—that was probably why he had jumped the fence.

When she finally got home, Natalie was annoyed to find that nobody else was around. The family car was gone, and she found a note inside saying they had all gone out to the grocery store. Natalie shrugged. Her sisters could be picky eaters, so her parents had probably wanted to make them choose something for dinner that they'd actually all eat.

They probably wouldn't be gone long, so Natalie decided to get ready to ride. When she led Tango out to the arena, she was irritated to find that someone—probably Emily or Grace—had left a small course of jumps set up. The rule was that after riding, everyone was supposed to clean up any equipment they had used. Natalie didn't want to leave Tango tied to the fence while she took down all the jumps, so she decided to just ride around them.

Her family still wasn't back by the time Natalie

had Tango tacked up. It didn't seem fair to make Tango stand around in his saddle and bridle for who knew how long, so she decided she'd get on and start warming up. Natalie was worried that Tango would be spooked by the brightly painted jumps, but he seemed more focused than usual. He walked, jogged, and loped obediently around the arena. His gaits were still too fast, but at least they were smooth.

Natalie turned Tango to reverse directions. Halfway across the arena, he veered off course and headed straight toward one of the jumps!

Natalie was so surprised that she didn't have time to react before Tango broke into a lope and jumped over the low red-and-white-striped jump. He landed smoothly and continued, reversing directions on his own. Just before reaching the rail, he gave a little hop that Natalie realized was a flying lead change.

At last, Natalie came to her senses and brought Tango back to a walk. Then she halted. Her mind was racing so fast that she was afraid she'd steer Tango into another jump without realizing it. Suddenly, everything that had been so mysterious about Tango made sense.

He was confused by her signals because he had been trained English, not Western! His gaits felt too fast because English horses were encouraged to move with long, sweeping strides. He was scared of cattle because he'd probably lived at a fancy lesson stable,

not a working ranch. And he could jump so well because that was probably what he did every day. The
flying change proved it—only a well-trained jumper
would have changed leads so smoothly after a jump
without even being asked.

To test her theory, Natalie held the rein in two
hands and steered Tango the English way. She closed
her hand around one rein and moved it slightly back
in the direction she wanted Tango to turn. Just like

she did when she was riding Western, she pressed her outside leg against his side.

Tango turned immediately. His neck and body curved gently into a smooth, tight circle. Natalie asked for another circle, this time neck reining. Tango made a wobbly egg-shaped loop.

There was no doubt about it: Tango was an English horse.

Natalie couldn't believe she hadn't thought of the possibility sooner. Sure, Western riding was more common in Texas, but lots of people rode English. Emily and Grace did, most of the time. And even though Natalie thought of Paints as a Western breed, she knew they could just as easily be used for English sports like jumping.

Natalie's racing thoughts were interrupted by the sound of the Ramirez family car pulling into the driveway. She felt a twinge of alarm—she had meant to dismount before her family got back, so they wouldn't know she'd been riding alone.

It was too late now. They had already seen her and were heading over across the yard. But instead of scolding, her parents and sisters were all smiles.

"Hurry up and come inside when you're finished riding," said her mother. "We've got a surprise for you."

Out of the corner of her eye, Natalie saw them carrying packages into the house that didn't look like groceries. But Natalie's mind was still working overtime as she led Tango back to the stable.

Did his English training mean that Natalie was going to have to switch to that kind of riding? She couldn't even imagine what her friends on the barrel-racing circuit would say if they saw her in the fancy show jacket and polished knee-high boots that English riders wore, loping—no, cantering—around a course of jumps covered in fake grass and flowers.

Natalie hardly remembered her family's promise of a surprise when she finished taking care of Tango and headed back to the house.

"Surprise!" cried Abby, and Natalie gasped when she saw the kitchen table covered in what looked like half the contents of a tack shop. There was a beautiful grooming box made of polished white pine, a set of brushes with natural soft-leather handles, a navy-blue horse blanket with silver buckles, and a silky red-white-and-blue braided lead rope that was much nicer than the old one Tango had come from the animal shelter with.

Best of all was a beautiful new Western show bridle, just like the one she'd had for Rockette, only this time for a full-size horse.

"It was all my idea!" said Grace, bouncing on her toes with excitement. "Instead of getting myself a new halter for Joker at the feed store, I decided to save my money and go to the fancy tack shop in Sassafras

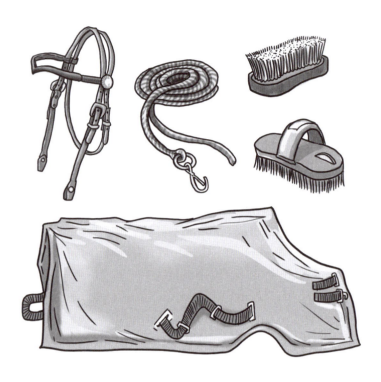

Springs to get new stuff for you and Tango. Except I only had nine dollars, but I told Emily and Abby, and they decided they'd spend their money too. Then we told Mom and Dad, and they bought you that bridle and lead rope and blanket, but the grooming kit is from Emily and Abby and me."

Grace paused for breath and went on: "And I wanted to get you this awesome bridle that was totally blinged-out with purple rhinestones, but Emily said you wouldn't appreciate it. So we picked out this one with just a little bit of silver on the browband. Do you love it?"

Natalie was speechless. She couldn't believe her family had been so thoughtful to surprise her like this. She went over and gave them each a big hug—first Grace, then Emily and Abby, and finally, each of her parents.

"I more than love it," she said when she could finally talk again. "It's all absolutely perfect. Thank you!"

Natalie brought Tango's beautiful new equipment out to the barn. She was so busy gazing at the silver engraving on the bridle that she nearly ran into Marco, who was feeding the horses.

"Oops, sorry!" she said, stopping just in time to avoid crashing into him.

He had a full water bucket in each hand, and Natalie knew from experience just how heavy they were. She couldn't help being impressed by how easily he carried them.

"That's some classy swag," he said with a grin, looking over Tango's new tack and brushes. "Hope that loco horse of yours appreciates it."

"Tango's not crazy, he—" For some reason, Natalie didn't want to admit that Tango had been trained English. It was almost like admitting he wasn't the right horse for her. "He just needs some time to adjust," she finished lamely.

"Maybe," said Marco, not sounding convinced. "Anyway, I meant to tell you yesterday, before that lovely horse of yours nearly broke your neck, that Pandora and me are going to be riding in the Tri-County Youth Rodeo on Saturday. Figured since you haven't been to one in a while, you might want to stop by and watch."

"Actually, I have—" Natalie stopped midsentence. A yoga class with Darcy? What was she thinking? Natalie wasn't any more interested in yoga than she was in learning to ride English instead of Western. Going to a rodeo might be just the inspiration Natalie needed to take Tango's training in a new direction.

"I mean, I'd love to go," said Natalie. "See you on Saturday!"

"Um, listen, Darcy, I'm not going to be able to make it to the yoga class on Saturday after all," said Natalie. The girls only had a few minutes in the hall before English class, but Natalie wanted to get this over with.

"Is everything okay?" asked Darcy, looking worried. "Is something wrong with one of your animals?"

"No, it's not that, it's just . . ." Natalie decided that honesty was the best approach, like jumping into a cold pool instead of edging into it inch by inch. "It's just that I was invited to go to a rodeo that day, and, well, that's kind of more my thing than yoga is."

"Oh, okay. . ." Darcy looked a little hurt, but she still smiled uncertainly. "Would you like to come over to my house on Sunday afternoon instead?"

Natalie took a big breath. "Actually, Darcy, I'm going to be pretty busy training Tango for a while. And I know you're not really into horses, so maybe it's better if we don't make plans to hang out right now." Her voice came out sounding rushed and awkward, like she was reading from a script.

Darcy's smile vanished. "Oh," she said. "I see."

The bell rang, and they went into class. Natalie didn't hear a word of what Ms. Coleman said about heroes and antiheroes in the book *Holes*. At lunch, Darcy joined a table on the opposite side of the cafeteria from where she and Natalie normally sat. She pulled out a notebook and started sketching something. She didn't even look in Natalie's direction.

Natalie sat with some other friends instead and tried to pay attention to their conversation about Izzy's older brother inviting Owen's older sister to a Reba Rodin concert in Dallas next month. Still, she couldn't stop herself from glancing over at Darcy every few minutes. She cringed when she saw Riley and Danica elbow each other, whisper something, and then move to take seats on either side of Darcy with fake, too-bright smiles.

But she guessed that wasn't really her problem now. Darcy was smart and nice, but she just wasn't cut out to be Natalie's best friend. Telling her sooner rather than later had been the right thing to do, Natalie was sure of it.

So why did it feel so wrong?

Chapter Eleven

There is nothing in the world as exciting as a *rodeo*, Natalie thought. The grounds rang out with the neighing of horses, the lowing of cattle, the muffled thunder of hoofbeats, and the shouting and cheering of cowboys and cowgirls. The smell of the rodeo was of leather, sweat, grit, trampled grass, and barbecue. The announcer's voice crackled over the loudspeaker, introducing the competitors and telling their times or scores for each event to the audience.

The excitement of the rodeo almost made Natalie forget about her conversation with Darcy the day before. Almost, but not quite. The image of Darcy's startled, disappointed face kept drifting into her head at random moments. But every time, she forced herself to push it right back out again and focus on the activity around her.

The whole Ramirez family had come to see the rodeo. They found Marco by the stock trailers with his chestnut quarter horse mare, Pandora. She looked alert and ready to go. Marco was competing in tie-down roping, which would be later that afternoon. Everyone wished him luck and then headed to the stands to find good seats.

The first event was bareback bronco riding. The

rider had to stay on the bucking horse for eight seconds, keeping one hand up in the air while spurring the horse on. Only about half of the riders stayed on for the full time.

After bareback riding came the saddle bronc competition, followed by steer wrestling. Then, a couple of rodeo hands rolled three big barrels into the arena and used a tape measure to set them up at specific distances apart. Natalie's heart quickened. If only she could be riding in this event today—on Tango!

The first competitor blazed into the arena at a flat-out gallop, activating the electric eye that started the timer. Natalie recognized Kate Graywolf, last year's Under-Eighteen State Champion, on her leopard Appaloosa gelding, Apocalypse.

Kate had won the title for a reason, and she didn't

disappoint today. Apocalypse galloped harder and turned tighter around the barrels than Natalie would have believed possible.

Twelve other riders competed in the event, but none of them came close to Kate's time. Natalie sighed with envy as Kate and Apocalypse galloped in a victory lap around the arena, holding up the engraved silver belt buckle she'd won as a prize.

Finally, it was time for the individual roping competition. Natalie watched the first three riders lasso their calves, throw them to the ground, and tie them, each rider faster than the last. Then it was Marco's turn.

He rode Pandora into the chute outside the arena. She was prancing in place with anticipation, jingling her bit in her mouth. The calf got a running start, and then Pandora was off like a shot. She caught up with the calf in a few bounding strides.

Marco let his lasso fly, and it fell neatly around the calf's neck. Pandora halted, and the rope tied to her saddle horn was pulled tight. The calf strained against it, but he wasn't nearly strong enough to break free. Marco threw the calf down and tied up three of its legs so fast that his hands were a blur. When he was finished, he threw his arms up into the air.

"Another record-beating time of thirteen-point-two seconds!" cried the announcer.

Marco ended up taking second place out of sixteen riders. "I'm happy with that," he said as the family went over to congratulate him. "The $500 in first-place prize money would have been nice, but our time was good enough to get us to the state semifinals."

In the car on the way home, Natalie thought back to the thrill of watching Kate Graywolf barrel race—and how hard it had been to just watch and not have a chance to compete herself.

Natalie hadn't realized just how much she'd missed it until now. And it would be a long time until Tango was ready to compete at that level. Her daydreams about winning the Under-Eighteen Championship seemed further away than ever. But it would all be worth it in the end, right?

The forecast was predicting a thunderstorm, so the family brought all the horses inside for the night. Natalie offered to do their evening feed by herself while her sisters helped take care of the other animals.

She had just dumped the last scoop of grain into the last feed bucket when she heard the phone ringing in the tack room. That was the business line for the ranch. Natalie ran to grab the phone before the caller hung up.

"Hello, you've reached Second Chance Ranch," she said, slightly out of breath.

"Hi, my name is Rachel Schwartz," said a voice

that sounded like a teenage girl. "I'm calling about a horse named Tango that I saw on your blog."

"Tango's not up for adoption, but we have a lot of others who are," said Natalie. "What kind of horse or pony are you looking for?"

"No, you don't understand," said the girl. "I'm not calling because I want to adopt a horse; I'm calling because mine was stolen. I'm Tango's owner."

Chapter Twelve

"**I understand you believe** that one of our horses belongs to you?" said Mr. Ramirez to the tall, dark-haired girl and her father, both of whom had shown up the next morning.

Natalie was glad her dad was there; she wasn't sure she could have talked to anyone at all right then.

Instead, she hung back and stared at the girl who claimed that Tango was hers. Rachel Schwartz looked about sixteen years old. She wore jeans, a cashmere sweater, and low English-style paddock boots. Her father was dressed in an expensive-looking business suit.

"We flew here from Florida this morning," said Rachel. "I have Tango's registration papers here—and some pictures."

Mr. Ramirez took the envelope she held out and looked over the contents. Natalie stepped forward and peered over his shoulder.

The papers were from the American Paint Horse Association, saying that Rachel Elizabeth Schwartz of Ocala, Florida, was the owner of an eight-year-old bay tobiano gelding named Two To Tango. Photos attached to the papers showed Rachel and a horse that was unmistakably Tango galloping bareback in

a pasture and jumping over a huge triple-bar fence. Finally, there was a close-up of his elegant head with a blue championship ribbon streaming from it.

Looking at them, Natalie felt so dizzy that she walked away and leaned against the apple tree in the yard for support. She took a few deep breaths to calm herself, but it still seemed like the world was spinning around her.

Tango didn't belong to Natalie at all. He really belonged to Rachel Schwartz of Ocala, Florida. Dimly, she could hear Rachel explaining the whole situation to Mr. Ramirez as he led her into the barn to see Tango.

It sounded like Rachel had been on her way to a big hunter-jumper show in California when Tango had gone missing from the trailer that was hired to haul him across the country. He had almost certainly been stolen, and the driver of the trailer was under suspicion for being in on it.

But there had been no evidence, no proof, and no sign of Tango for three months—until Rachel's friend had shared a link to the Second Chance Ranch blog on her social media account, and Rachel had seen Tango's picture.

Still half-hoping she might wake up from this bad dream, Natalie trudged into the barn. Emily and Grace were there, talking to Rachel and oohing and aahing over the pictures of Tango jumping.

"How high are those fences?" asked Grace.

"Three foot six," said Rachel. "That's the height of the working hunter division that Tango and I show in. He can jump higher, though, so I might switch over to open-jumper classes next year. Those fences can be over five feet tall!"

"Wow," said Grace breathlessly. "I've only ever jumped two feet, but I love to see people riding over big fences. Would you ride Tango for us now? My sister was trying to turn him into a barrel-racing horse. Isn't that funny? And he's scared of cows!"

Rachel laughed and started to tell a story about Tango refusing to enter the show ring at a Tri-County Fair because he had seen llamas there that morning. But Natalie didn't stick around to hear the end of it. She ran past the tack room and up the ladder to the hayloft—her refuge when she wanted to be alone. She climbed up onto a big pile of round bales and lay down in a patch of sunlight.

Through the small window in the loft, she could see Rachel lead Tango into the arena wearing English tack. A few minutes later, she was jumping him over a course of jumps Grace had set up.

He didn't seem skittish or confused now; he looked powerful and confident. He leaped over the jumps as if he could easily clear something twice as high. When he landed, his bright eyes searched out the next fence.

Natalie turned away from the window and let

herself cry like she'd wanted to since she'd picked up the phone the day before. She hadn't really believed that Tango would be taken away from her—until now.

"Natalie?" said a soft voice from below.

Natalie rolled over and peered over the edge of the hay bales. Emily was staring up at her, her blue eyes filled with sympathy.

"I just wanted to let you know that Rachel and her dad left. They'll be back tomorrow," she said softly. "And, um, I'm really sorry about Tango. I know how special he is to you."

Natalie couldn't say anything. She just nodded.

"Is there anything I can do?" asked Emily. "Do you want me to bring you a kitten? Kittens always make me feel better when I'm sad."

"No thanks," said Natalie, smiling weakly in spite of herself. "I think I just feel like being alone right now."

Emily nodded and quietly walked away. Natalie stayed in the sweet-smelling hay for a moment, then wiped her eyes on her sleeve and headed down to the barn to see Tango.

He hung his head over the half-door of his stall and snuffled her hands curiously to see if she had any treats. But Natalie didn't feel as if he was really looking for her. He never had been. He'd always been looking a little bit beyond her, at something in the distance.

Now she knew he'd been waiting for his real owner to find him. At first, Natalie felt only pain, remembering how magnificent Tango had looked with Rachel riding him. But something about seeing him like that made Natalie feel a strange joy, even as the sadness of losing him felt so overwhelming. Maybe one day Tango could be a good barrel horse—but he was already a great jumper.

"I guess that owning you would have to make one of us into something that we're not," she murmured, stroking Tango's soft nose.

Natalie's words echoed in her head, and suddenly, she realized that she'd made almost the exact same mistake with Darcy.

She had expected Darcy to be like Sophia, just like she'd expected Tango to fit the image of the perfect barrel-racing horse she had in her head. When things hadn't turned out that way, she'd just ignored all the evidence instead of facing the truth.

Natalie knew that she wasn't cut out for English riding because she'd tried it before. But Natalie hadn't given yoga or sushi or any of the stuff Darcy liked a chance. Maybe Natalie would even have enjoyed that weird French movie if she'd asked Darcy what was going on instead of sulking because they weren't watching what Natalie and Sophia would have watched.

Darcy wasn't Sophia—she was Darcy. She was funny and creative and helpful, and Natalie liked her, pink clothing and allergies and all. But could she find a way to explain all this to Darcy after Natalie's rude behavior the week before? Would Darcy even want to hear it?

Chapter Thirteen

Natalie took a deep breath and walked up to the cafeteria table where Darcy was sitting with Riley and Danica.

"Can I talk to you for a minute?" she said to Darcy, who wasn't wearing anything pink today, just jeans and a black T-shirt—and earrings shaped like running giraffes.

"Maybe she doesn't want to talk to you," said Danica, narrowing her eyes and taking a swig from the giant bottle of diet Mountain Dew that she always toted around.

But Darcy looked at Natalie and said, "Talk to me about what?"

"Um, I was just going to get some candy at the vending machines," said Natalie. "Come with me?"

Darcy shrugged and stood up. "I'll be back in a minute," she said to the other girls, who raised their eyebrows but said nothing.

Natalie didn't really want any candy. She'd just been looking for an excuse to get Darcy away from Riley and Danica. She put a dollar into the machine and punched a random button. She ended up with a Snickers bar. She tore open the wrapper, broke it in half, and offered half to Darcy.

Darcy shook her head. "I'm allergic to peanuts," she said. "So, what is it that you wanted to say to me?"

Natalie stared down at the gooey chocolate in her hand and tried to think of how to explain. "You know how sometimes you try on an outfit in a store and it looks perfect, then you take it home and you realize it's just not working at all?" she said.

Darcy looked at Natalie warily.

"Well, sometimes it's the opposite—you try on something that isn't your usual style, so you don't buy it," said Natalie. "And then you get home, and you realize how cool and unique it actually was."

Natalie knew she should stop there. But she didn't. "So you rush back to the store, only to find that someone really annoying has already bought the wonderful outfit, and you just know they're going to spill diet Mountain Dew on it eventually and ruin it, and that makes you really sad."

Darcy didn't laugh. But the corner of her mouth twitched.

"And, um, I guess that's how I feel. I mean, not that friendship is like a piece of clothing you can buy. It's just, you know . . ."

"Yeah," said Darcy. "I get it." She glanced across the room at Riley and Danica, who were staring closely at them. When Darcy caught them at it, they didn't even look away or pretend to be interested in something else.

"So, is that, like, an apology?" asked Darcy, turning back to Natalie.

"Yes, it definitely is," said Natalie.

"Then it's accepted, I guess."

Natalie let out the breath that she didn't realize she'd been holding. "Great! And, um . . . I'd like to try that yoga class, if you wanted to invite me again sometime."

"Really?" said Darcy.

"On one condition," said Natalie.

"What's that?"

"You promise to watch an entire episode of *Zombie High* before you decide whether you like it or not."

Darcy nodded. "Okay," she said, "I will. But just so you know, Riley and Danica have been pretty nice to me so far, and I'm probably going to still be friends with them too."

"Sure, no problem," said Natalie. "As long as I don't have to hang out with them too."

Darcy laughed at that and then headed back to her table, where Riley and Danica immediately started peppering her with questions. Natalie grimaced. But Darcy had the right to be friends with Riley and Danica if she wanted—as hard as it was to put all those words in the same sentence.

And just like Natalie's problem hadn't really been with Darcy, the same thing might be true for Sophia. Natalie had only ever had one close friend before, but it didn't have to be that way. It wasn't like friendship was a rodeo event where only one winner could take home the prize money.

The whole idea of a "best" friend sounded a little silly when Natalie thought about it that way. How could you compare one person to another?

Later that evening, Natalie called up Sophia on FaceTime. She told her all about the animals that had been adopted at the open house and then about Rachel Schwartz and Tango.

"I'm sorry it didn't end up working out, but I know you'll find the perfect horse soon," said Sophia. "And look on the bright side: Now you've got all this great tack and equipment when you finally *do* find your super horse!"

"That's true," said Natalie. Then she took a deep breath. "So there's this new girl at school—Darcy—that I've been hanging out with a lot lately," she said.

"Oh yeah? What's she like?" asked Sophia.

"Well, she's a little quiet at first but really funny once you get to know her. And she's got a great sense of style. She's not too adventurous about spicy food, though. I made our infamous quadruple-alarm nachos, and she would barely even taste them."

"She sounds cool," said Sophia. "Maybe you'll be able to toughen up her taste buds."

"Well, that still hasn't worked with Abby yet," said Natalie. She paused for a moment. "You don't mind, do you?"

"No, why would I?" asked Sophia, sounding puzzled.

"Well, quadruple-alarm nachos were kind of *our* thing. I thought you might be upset that I shared them with someone else," Natalie admitted.

Sophia laughed. "Actually, I've been feeling kind of bad that you seem so lonely since I left. I mean, I'm sad that I had to move, too, and I miss you, and I'm glad you feel the same way . . . but I don't want you to be sad and missing me all the time, you know?"

"Yeah, I do," said Natalie, realizing she felt the same way about Sophia's new friends.

"So, in other news, I can't believe you were right about Harper on *Zombie High*!" said Sophia. "But what was up with that shot of the paw prints outside the principal's office?"

"Oh, that's so obvious. The new principal is clearly not a zombie; he's a werewolf."

"*What*?"

"I'm sure of it. There have been hints all season . . ."

By the time they said good night half an hour later, all of Natalie's hurt and jealousy had melted away. Well, almost. Natalie still wished she could see Sophia at school every day. But the things that Natalie liked best about Sophia would never change, no matter how many miles were between them.

Chapter Fourteen

Natalie swallowed hard as she heard the sound of a heavy vehicle crunching down the gravel driveway. She gave Tango a final swipe with the glossy mahogany-handled body brush her sisters had given her and then set it down in her new grooming box as Rachel and her dad walked into the barn.

"He's all ready for you," she said to Rachel, trying to keep her voice steady.

"He looks wonderful!" said Rachel. "I brought his shipping boots too." She held up a pair of burgundy leg protectors lined with white fleece.

Natalie helped fasten them onto Tango's legs. Then, before she lost her cool, she gave Tango a final brisk pat and handed his lead rope to Rachel. She'd already decided that she wasn't going to cry.

She lingered a few steps behind as Rachel led Tango out of the barn and toward the ramp of a sleek silver trailer hitched up to a black SUV.

Tango didn't hesitate. In fact, when he saw it, he broke into a jog—a trot, really; he was an English horse, after all. He looked back just once, his face alert and his nostrils flaring, as if he were taking in the sights and smells of the ranch one last time. It seemed to Natalie that his eyes fixed on her for an extra-long moment—or maybe she was imagining it. Then he swung his head back around and walked briskly up the ramp.

Rachel ducked out of a small side door on the trailer and then shut the back with a final-sounding *clang*.

She came over to join her father, who was taking a check out of his sleek leather wallet. He held it out to Natalie. "Here's a small donation to help cover the cost of Tango's care," he said.

Natalie glanced down as she reached for it. The check was for $5,000!

"Oh, this is too much," said Natalie. "Keeping Tango for a few weeks wasn't nearly that expensive."

"It's the least we can do after you've taken such good care of him," he said, insisting that Natalie take the check.

"Thank you," Rachel added.

"You're welcome," said Natalie. "I'm glad you found Tango."

And she meant it. She still thought Tango was pretty much the perfect horse—just not the perfect horse for *her*. She'd find that horse someday, though.

"Now round your spine and stretch up into cat pose," said the yoga instructor over a soundtrack of flute music and water running over stones.

Natalie followed his instructions, imagining that she was Autumn, rising from a long nap in her favorite spot on the sunny living room windowsill.

Natalie didn't think that yoga would ever become part of her Saturday morning routine, but the class was sort of fun. And it ended with something called "corpse pose," which Natalie thought was kind of cool, because it reminded her of *Zombie High*.

"I can't believe you could do that crazy pose standing on your elbows," she said to Darcy after the class was over.

"You mean feathered peacock pose? Yeah, that's a tricky one," said Darcy. "It took months of classes before I could hold my balance for more than a few seconds."

Darcy might not be very good at basketball, but she was definitely athletic in her own way. Natalie had toppled immediately and awkwardly to the ground when she'd tried the handstand pose that Darcy seemed to do so effortlessly.

The yoga studio was within walking distance of Darcy's apartment, and the girls headed back there together. Darcy and her mom lived on the second floor above a law office, and their living room bay window had a great view of Main Street. The apartment was small but decorated in a way that made it seem bigger. Maybe it was because there was so much interesting stuff to look at: plants, paintings, sculptures, and lots of books on a shelf that was built like a staircase along one whole wall.

Ms. Chang made lunch for them: a fancy salad with goat cheese, sunflower seeds, and cranberries. Again, it wasn't the sort of thing that Natalie would fix for herself, but it was interesting.

And Darcy's cat was *definitely* interesting. At first, Natalie was shocked by the sight of the hairless cat. With her wrinkled pink-and-gray skin, Cleopatra looked like a newborn rabbit from the nest that Natalie had once found in the horse pasture. But she purred when Natalie petted her strange, smooth skin, and she played with her catnip mouse just like Autumn did.

Darcy's whole face lit up as she laughed at Cleopatra's antics, and Natalie realized that Darcy really did love animals as much as she did. She was glad that Darcy had found a pet that she could play with and cuddle without having to worry about allergies.

When Cleopatra tired of entertaining her audience, Darcy showed Natalie her sketchbook filled with ideas for outfits she'd like to create someday. Then she flipped to the last page and showed Natalie a picture of some horses in a pasture. Not just any horses, Natalie realized—it was the herd at Second Chance Ranch.

Just like he had been on the day Darcy had visited, Tango was standing a short distance from the herd, looking off to the horizon with his head held high. The picture was so lifelike that Natalie half-expected to hear his familiar neigh.

Darcy had gotten the pattern of Tango's coat and the other horses' markings almost exactly right.

"That's amazing!" Natalie breathed, tracing her finger lightly over Tango's Paint markings and flowing tail.

Darcy blushed. "Yeah, I've always had kind of a photographic memory. But I could do a better job if I were sketching *plein air*—that means outside, from life. Maybe I could come back to the farm sometime and do more sketches of the animals. I mean, if you wanted to auction them off or something, maybe it could help raise money for the ranch. And I thought you might like to have this picture for yourself, to remember Tango."

If Natalie had any doubts whether she and Darcy had enough in common, they vanished right then. Liking the same movies and food and clothes was nice, but it wasn't important. Darcy was a friend in every way that mattered.

"Hey, want to give each other manicures?" asked Darcy. "I just got some new nail polish—Mod Midnight Blue!"

Somehow, Natalie had lived twelve and a half years on this earth without ever painting her nails midnight blue. But that was going to end today.

"Sure! Why not?" she said. "And you know what we're going to do after that?"

"What?" asked Darcy.

Natalie dug through the clothes in her sleepover bag and pulled out the complete first season of *Zombie High* on DVD. "We're going to watch the best show ever!"

About the Author

Whitney Sanderson grew up riding horses as a member of a 4-H club and competing in local jumping and dressage shows. She has written several books in the Horse Diaries chapter book series. She is also the author of *Horse Rescue: Treasure*, based on her time volunteering at an equine rescue farm. She lives in Massachusetts.

About the Illustrator

Jomike Tejido is an author and illustrator who has illustrated the books *I Funny: School of Laughs* and *Middle School: Dog's Best Friend*, as well as the Pet Charms and I Want to Be . . . Dinosaurs! series. He has fond memories of horseback riding as a kid and has always liked drawing fluffy animals. Jomike lives in Manila with his wife, his daughter Sophia, and a chow chow named Oso.